Cosmic Melodies; A Duet Of Love And Discovery

Mrigendra Bharti

Published by Sellbrochure Vymish Entertainment, 2024.

This is a work of fiction. Similarities to real people, places, or events are entirely coincidental.

COSMIC MELODIES; A DUET OF LOVE AND DISCOVERY

First edition. July 9, 2024.

ISBN: 979-8227064677

Written by Mrigendra Bharti.

Table of Contents

Preface

Have you ever gazed at the starlit sky and felt a sense of awe and wonder? Have you ever wondered if there's more to the universe than meets the eye, a hidden melody waiting to be discovered?

This book is an invitation to explore that very notion. It's the story of Ethan, a young astrophysicist consumed by the mysteries of the cosmos, and Olivia, a passionate musician whose soul yearns to translate the universe's beauty into music.

Their paths collide amidst the towering shelves of a library, their initial awkward encounters blossoming into a love story unlike any other. As their connection deepens, they realize that science and art aren't opposing forces, but rather two sides of the same coin. Ethan's research finds new meaning through the evocative language of Olivia's music, while her compositions gain depth and precision through his scientific lens.

This book isn't just a love story; it's a journey of exploration, a testament to the power of collaboration. It follows Ethan and Olivia as they navigate the challenges of ambition and the uncertainties of life, their love story serving as a constant source of strength and inspiration.

As you delve into the pages that follow, prepare to be transported to a world where scientific theories dance with musical notes, where constellations inspire symphonies, and where the vast expanse of the universe becomes a canvas for love and discovery.

Let "Cosmic Melodies; A Duet of Love and Discovery" ignite your own sense of wonder and remind you that the greatest discoveries often lie at the intersection of science, art, and the enduring melody of the human spirit.

Prologue

The crisp autumn air of New England carried a faint scent of nostalgia as a young woman with fiery red hair hurried through the bustling campus of Elyria Academy. Olivia clutched a worn leather-bound notebook in her hand, its pages filled with scribbled musical notes and celestial sketches. A melody danced in her mind, a complex symphony mirroring the swirling galaxies and nebulae she'd spent countless nights studying.

Reaching the library, a haven of towering shelves and hushed whispers, Olivia made her way towards the astronomy section. A shy smile played on her lips as she spotted him in the corner, his brow furrowed in concentration. Ethan, a handsome young man with dark hair perpetually ruffled, was surrounded by astronomy texts, his eyes glued to a complex diagram.

Olivia hesitated for a moment, the melody in her head faltering. Their connection, borne out of stolen glances and whispered conversations amidst the library stacks, hadn't yet blossomed into something more. Yet, an undeniable pull drew her towards him, a silent understanding that their shared fascination with the universe might bridge the gap between them.

Taking a deep breath, Olivia walked over to Ethan, her notebook clutched tightly. As she approached, he looked up, his initial surprise melting into a warm smile. In that shared glance, under the watchful gaze of constellations etched on ancient maps, their love story, a symphony yet to be played, found its first note.

About Sellbrochure
Vymish
Entertainment

Sellbrochure Vymish Entertainment, recognized as India's largest book publishing company, has made significant strides in ensuring its extensive collection of books reaches audiences across the global market. This rapid expansion is a testament to the company's dedication to disseminating knowledge and literature far beyond national borders. Central to its success is its affiliation with InkWhirl Media Networks, a reputable entity in the media and publication industry known for its innovative and strategic approaches. Within this network, InkWhirl Publication LLC operates as a vital division, further enhancing the company's capabilities and reach in the international market.

The visionary behind this enterprise is Mrigendra Bharti, the founder of Sellbrochure Vymish Entertainment. His foresight and passion for the literary world have been instrumental in steering the company towards remarkable growth and recognition. Under his leadership, Sellbrochure Vymish Entertainment has not only expanded its catalog but also established a strong presence in both domestic and international markets. Mrigendra Bharti's commitment to excellence and innovation has been a driving force in the company's journey, ensuring that it stays ahead of industry trends and meets the evolving needs of readers worldwide.

Sellbrochure Vymish Entertainment operates under the robust support of its parental organization, Mrigendra Bharti Group InfoTech. This affiliation provides the necessary resources and strategic guidance, enabling the publishing company to undertake ambitious projects and explore new markets. Mrigendra Bharti Group InfoTech's extensive experience in technology and information services has been a valuable asset, allowing Sellbrochure Vymish Entertainment to integrate advanced digital solutions in its operations, thereby enhancing its distribution capabilities and reader engagement.

Through relentless efforts and a commitment to quality, Sellbrochure Vymish Entertainment continues to break barriers and expand the reach of Indian literature globally. The company's diverse portfolio includes a wide range of genres, catering to different age groups and interests, thereby fostering a rich and inclusive reading culture. As it continues to innovate and grow, Sellbrochure Vymish Entertainment remains dedicated to its mission of making literature accessible to all, contributing significantly to the global literary landscape.

Connect With Mrigendra,
Thank you very much for choosing this book.
You can also connect with me on Instagram,
https://www.instagram.com/i_mrigendrabharti.official
With Love,
Mrigendra Bharti

Introduction

The universe, a vast and ever-expanding tapestry woven with stardust and swirling galaxies, has long held the power to ignite human imagination. From the cradle of civilization, humankind has gazed at the night sky, seeking answers to life's greatest mysteries. But what if the secrets of the cosmos weren't confined to cold equations and astronomical charts? What if the language of the universe could be translated not just through scientific inquiry, but also through the evocative power of music?

This is the story of Ethan and Olivia, two souls whose paths intertwined amidst the towering shelves of a grand library. Ethan, a brilliant astrophysicist consumed by the mysteries of dark matter and the birth of stars, dreamt of unraveling the universe's grand design. Olivia, a passionate musician with a fiery spirit, yearned to capture the celestial beauty in melodic form.

Their initial encounter was a spark, a chance meeting amidst a sea of books that ignited a connection far deeper than shared academic interests. Ethan found himself captivated by Olivia's boundless curiosity and the way she saw music woven into the very fabric of the cosmos. Olivia, in turn, was drawn to Ethan's unwavering dedication to scientific exploration and the way his passion for research mirrored her own artistic fervor.

This isn't simply a love story set against the backdrop of a university library; it's a tale of synergy, a testament to the power of collaboration. As Ethan and Olivia delve deeper into their respective pursuits, they discover that science and art aren't opposing forces, but rather complementary parts of a larger whole. Ethan's research finds new meaning through the evocative language of music, while Olivia's compositions gain depth and precision through his scientific lens.

Their journey takes them from stargazing sessions under a canopy of twinkling stars to prestigious academic conferences, each step along the way a testament to their unwavering support for each other's dreams. But as their careers flourish, a new challenge emerges – the delicate balance between individual ambition and the nurturing of their shared passion.

Prepare to embark on a journey of discovery, where scientific theories dance with musical notes, where constellations inspire symphonies, and where the vast expanse of the universe becomes a canvas for love and a testament to the boundless potential that unfolds when hearts and minds dare to dream together. This is "Cosmic Melodies; A Duet of Love and Discovery," a story that will leave you with a renewed sense of wonder and a belief in the power of human connection to unlock the universe's greatest mysteries.

Chapter 1: The Enigmatic Ethan and the Radiant Olivia

Elyria City, a bustling metropolis pulsating with energy and ambition, was home to Elyria Academy, a majestic institution that stood as a testament to the pursuit of knowledge. Its gothic architecture, a stark contrast to the surrounding contemporary skyscrapers, whispered tales of a bygone era. Within its ivy-clad walls resided a vibrant ecosystem of scholars – a melting pot of aspiring minds, each brimming with dreams of leaving their mark on the world. The hallowed halls echoed with the symphony of youthful voices, punctuated by the rhythmic tap of textbooks against desks and the hushed murmurs of scholarly debates. In this intellectual milieu thrived Ethan Moore, a young man whose brilliance outshone even the most polished diamonds.

Ethan's dark brown hair, perpetually unruly as if defying gravity's constraints, framed a face that held the captivating glint of boundless curiosity. He was the epitome of academic prowess, his mind a labyrinthine repository of facts, figures, and philosophical theories. Textbooks were his companions, libraries his sanctuaries, and complex equations his puzzles to solve. He devoured knowledge with an insatiable hunger, his thirst for understanding seemingly unquenchable.

Yet, beneath Ethan's unassuming exterior lay an ocean of untapped emotions. He possessed a quiet charm, a gentle demeanor that belied the intensity of his thoughts. He yearned for a connection that transcended the sterile pages of his textbooks, a bond that resonated with the depths of his soul. However, social interactions were an enigma to Ethan. He navigated the treacherous waters of human connection with the grace of a newborn giraffe, his brilliance often overshadowed by his awkward silences and nervous stumbles.

One crisp autumn morning, as the first rays of dawn painted the sky in a breathtaking tapestry of gold and rose, Ethan found himself ensconced in his usual haunt – the academy's grand library. The air hung heavy with the comforting scent of aged paper and leather bindings, a familiar fragrance that soothed his soul. He was meticulously dissecting a particularly perplexing physics theorem, his brow furrowed in concentration as he meticulously scratched calculations on a dusty chalkboard. Suddenly, a cascade of melodious notes drifted through the air, shattering the tranquil silence of the library.

The music, a hauntingly beautiful melody played on a piano, was unlike anything Ethan had ever heard before. It was an ethereal blend of classical grace and contemporary flair, the notes weaving a tapestry of emotions that resonated deep within him. Curiosity piqued, Ethan abandoned his equations and embarked on a quest to find the source of this captivating melody. He tiptoed through the labyrinthine corridors of the library, his heart pounding a frantic rhythm against his ribs. The music grew louder, guiding him towards a hidden alcove nestled amidst towering bookshelves.

As Ethan rounded the corner, his breath hitched. There, bathed in the warm glow of a solitary table lamp, sat a vision unlike any he had ever encountered. Her fingers danced gracefully across the ivory keys of a grand piano, her back towards him. Her fiery red hair, cascading down her shoulders like a waterfall of molten lava, seemed to shimmer with every note she played. Her posture exuded an aura of effortless elegance, yet a hint of vulnerability peeked through in the way she bit her lower lip in concentration. Ethan stood mesmerized, captivated not only by her musical prowess but by the raw emotion that poured forth from her fingertips.

In that stolen moment, amidst the symphony of notes and the quietude of the library, a spark ignited. A connection, as invisible yet undeniable as gravity, formed between two souls as different as night and day, yet drawn together by an invisible thread of destiny. Their paths had finally crossed, and the story of the star-crossed lovers of Elyria Academy was about to begin.

Ethan remained rooted to the spot, a silent observer in the face of this unexpected muse. The music flowed from Olivia's fingertips like a torrent of emotions, each note a brushstroke painting a vivid picture in the canvas of silence. It spoke of a yearning for something more, a dissatisfaction with the ordinary, a sentiment that resonated deeply within Ethan himself.

As the final notes faded into a melancholic whisper, the library plunged back into an almost oppressive silence. Olivia, unaware of Ethan's presence, sat motionless for a moment, her eyes closed, lost in the afterglow of the music she had created. Ethan, his heart still pounding a frantic rhythm against his ribs, debated whether to make his presence known. He was a creature of logic and reason, yet this encounter defied all his usual calculations.

Finally, a deep breath and a gentle cough escaped his lips. Olivia's eyes snapped open, startled, and she spun around on the piano bench, her fiery red hair whipping around her face like a flame. Her emerald eyes, wide with surprise, landed on Ethan, and a flicker of recognition passed between them.

"Oh! I, uh," Olivia stammered, a blush creeping up her neck. "I didn't realize anyone was here."

Ethan, ever the scholar, fumbled for the appropriate words. "The music," he managed, his voice barely a hoarse whisper. "It was...beautiful."

A relieved smile spread across Olivia's face. "Thank you," she said, her voice soft and melodic. "I'm Olivia, by the way."

"Ethan," he replied, extending a hand towards her. Olivia's handshake was firm and surprisingly strong, a hint of the fire that resided within her.

As they exchanged introductions, a chasm seemed to separate their worlds. Ethan, with his rumpled clothes and nose perpetually buried in a book, was the epitome of the studious academic. Olivia, on the other hand, radiated an artistic flair, her crimson hair and unconventional style a stark contrast to the muted tones favored by most students.

Despite their differences, a sense of curiosity crackled between them. Ethan, ever the intellectual, was intrigued by the emotional depth Olivia poured into her music. Olivia, in turn, found herself drawn to Ethan's quiet intensity, the hidden depths that lurked beneath his unassuming exterior.

"So, what are you working on?" Olivia asked, gesturing towards the abandoned chalkboard.

Ethan cleared his throat. "Just a little something on advanced physics," he mumbled, suddenly self-conscious about his academic pursuits.

Olivia's eyes widened with surprise. "Wow, advanced physics? That sounds...complex."

Ethan, relieved to be on familiar ground, launched into an explanation of the theorem he had been grappling with. He spoke with a passion that belied his usual reserved nature, his hands gesturing animatedly as he explained the intricate concepts. Olivia listened intently, her brow furrowed in concentration as she tried to follow his train of thought.

Despite the technical jargon, Olivia found herself captivated by Ethan's enthusiasm. She had never met anyone who could talk about physics with such fervor, who could make complex equations seem like a thrilling adventure. As Ethan spoke, a new facet of his personality emerged – a hidden wellspring of passion that contradicted his bookish exterior.

Their conversation flowed effortlessly, traversing the vast landscapes that separated their academic disciplines. Ethan learned about Olivia's love for art, her dreams of becoming a renowned pianist, and her desire to use her music to evoke emotions in others. Olivia, in turn, discovered Ethan's fascination with the cosmos, his insatiable curiosity about the universe's mysteries, and his secret yearning for a deeper connection.

As the morning sun climbed higher in the sky, casting its warm rays through the library windows, they realized they had spent hours lost in conversation. Time had seemed to melt away, the silence of the library replaced by the symphony of their shared thoughts and dreams.

Theirs was an unlikely friendship, a bridge built between two seemingly disparate worlds. Yet, in that shared space, amidst the towering shelves and the scent of aged paper, a connection had blossomed, a foundation laid for a story that promised to be anything but ordinary.

The unexpected encounter in the library marked a turning point in Ethan and Olivia's lives. Their initial awkwardness melted away, replaced by a sense of comfortable camaraderie.

They began to seek each other out, drawn together by an invisible force that transcended their differences.

Ethan, who usually spent his free time buried in textbooks in the library's secluded corners, now found himself drawn to the music room. He would sit mesmerized, bathed in the warm glow emanating from the grand piano, as Olivia's fingers danced across the ivories, weaving tales of joy and sorrow through her music. He discovered a newfound appreciation for the arts, his logical mind captivated by the emotional language Olivia spoke through her music.

Olivia, in turn, started venturing into the library during her breaks. She would watch Ethan from afar, a smile playing on her lips as he meticulously scribbled calculations on a whiteboard, his brow furrowed in concentration. His passion for knowledge, once a solitary pursuit, became a shared experience. She found herself enjoying the intellectual stimulation of their conversations, her artistic spirit intrigued by the vast universe Ethan unveiled through his scientific explanations.

Their lunchtime rendezvous became a cherished routine. They would steal away to a secluded corner of the cafeteria, a haven amidst the bustling student body. Ethan, usually a quiet observer, would come alive as he shared his latest scientific discoveries, his voice animated with excitement. Olivia, an eager listener, would pepper him with questions, her curiosity a constant challenge to his knowledge.

One crisp autumn afternoon, as they sat huddled over a worn copy of astronomy, Ethan pointed towards a diagram of the Milky Way galaxy. "Imagine," he said, his voice filled with awe, "billions of stars, each with its own story to tell."

Olivia's gaze followed his finger, her emerald eyes reflecting the wonder he felt. "It's mind-boggling," she whispered, a shiver running down her spine. "And yet, here we are, just two specks of dust in this vast universe."

A comfortable silence descended upon them, a shared sense of awe binding them closer. In that moment, amidst the constellations etched on the page and the whispered secrets of the universe, Ethan realized he craved more than intellectual companionship with Olivia. He yearned for a deeper connection, a bond that resonated with the very core of his being.

As they walked back to their respective classes after lunch, a golden hue bathed the academy grounds in a warm glow. Ethan stole a glance at Olivia, her fiery hair catching the sunlight like a halo. He felt a surge of nervous energy coursing through him, a desire to bridge the gap between friendship and something more.

Suddenly, Olivia stopped walking, her gaze fixed on a flyer plastered on a bulletin board. "An astronomy club meeting?" she exclaimed, her voice filled with excitement. "Tonight? We have to go!"

Ethan's heart skipped a beat. Here was his chance, an opportunity to spend time with Olivia outside the confines of the academy. "Sure," he stammered, a blush creeping up his neck. "I mean, if you'd like me to come with you."

Olivia's smile was radiant. "I'd love that," she said, her eyes sparkling with anticipation.

As they walked side-by-side towards their classes, a silent pact had been formed. The stars, once a distant curiosity for Ethan, now held a new significance. They were a symbol of the connection blossoming between him and Olivia, a promise of a future filled with shared experiences and whispered secrets under the vast canvas of the night sky. The academy library, once a sanctuary of solitude for Ethan, had become the unlikely setting for an extraordinary encounter. It was there, amidst the towering shelves and the scent of aged paper, that a love story, as unique and captivating as the stars themselves, had begun to unfold.

The prospect of attending the astronomy club meeting together filled Ethan with a nervous excitement that rivaled the thrill of unraveling a complex scientific theory. Here was a chance to spend time with Olivia outside the familiar confines of the library and cafeteria, to explore a shared interest beyond the walls of their academic disciplines.

As the day progressed, Ethan found himself fidgeting in his classes, his mind constantly drifting back to the evening ahead. He meticulously planned his outfit, a compromise between his usual rumpled attire and a level of presentability that wouldn't send Olivia fleeing. He practiced conversation starters in his head, discarding one cliche after another in his quest for the perfect opening line.

By the time the final bell rang, signaling the end of the school day, Ethan was a bundle of nervous energy. He met Olivia outside the library, their eyes meeting in a silent acknowledgment of the unspoken anticipation simmering between them.

The astronomy club meeting was held in a small, observatory-like building perched atop a distant hill overlooking the academy. As they climbed the winding path, the cityscape sprawled beneath them, a glittering tapestry of twinkling lights. The crisp autumn air carried the distant rumble of the city, a stark contrast to the peaceful serenity that enveloped the observatory.

Inside, the room buzzed with the excited chatter of students gathered around telescopes and star charts. Ethan, initially overwhelmed by the unfamiliar territory, found himself drawn in by Olivia's infectious enthusiasm. She introduced him to the club members, her voice brimming with pride as she explained his interest in astronomy, a subject she had only recently discovered through their conversations.

Throughout the meeting, Ethan found himself captivated not just by the celestial wonders projected onto the screen but also by the way Olivia's eyes lit up as she learned about distant galaxies and nebulas. He reveled in her genuine curiosity, her thirst for knowledge mirroring his own.

After the presentations, the club members ventured outside, eager to train their telescopes on the night sky. Ethan, with Olivia by his side, fumbled with the unfamiliar equipment, his initial awkwardness quickly dissolving under her patient guidance.

As they peered through the telescope, the vast expanse of the universe unfolded before them. Ethan pointed out constellations, his voice filled with newfound confidence as he shared his knowledge. Olivia listened intently, her eyes wide with wonder as she absorbed the information.

In that moment, bathed in the soft glow of the Milky Way, a comfortable silence descended upon them. It was a silence filled with unspoken understanding, a shared appreciation for the universe's magnificent secrets. The awkwardness that had initially marked their interactions had melted away, replaced by a sense of camaraderie that transcended their differences.

As the night wore on, and the stars began their descent towards the horizon, Ethan and Olivia found themselves lingering by the telescope, lost in a conversation that flowed effortlessly. They talked about their dreams and aspirations, their fears and vulnerabilities, a level of intimacy they hadn't shared with anyone else.

The walk back to the academy was filled with a comfortable silence, punctuated by occasional bursts of laughter. There was a newfound ease in their interactions, a sense of familiarity that belied the brevity of their acquaintance.

As they reached the library, where their unlikely encounter had begun just days ago, Olivia turned to Ethan, a hesitant smile gracing her lips.

"Thank you for tonight, Ethan," she said, her voice soft. "It was...magical."

Ethan's heart soared. "For me too, Olivia," he stammered, his voice thick with emotion. "More than magical."

In that shared moment, under the watchful gaze of the moon, the foundation of a friendship bloomed. A friendship built on mutual respect, intellectual curiosity, and a spark of something deeper, a connection that promised to illuminate their lives in ways they never imagined. The stars, once distant celestial bodies, now held a new meaning for Ethan and Olivia. They were a testament to the extraordinary journey that had begun, a silent promise of a future filled with shared adventures and whispered secrets under the vast canvas of the night sky.

Chapter 2: Unveiling Hidden Feelings and Navigating Societal Expectations

Days turned into weeks, and the bond between Ethan and Olivia blossomed with the tenacity of a vine winding itself around a sturdy oak. Their friendship transcended the confines of the astronomy club and spilled over into every aspect of their academic lives. They found themselves drawn to each other's classes, Ethan sitting patiently through lectures on music theory, his gaze occasionally straying towards Olivia, captivated by her animated interactions with the professor. Olivia, in turn, would appear at Ethan's physics lectures, her brow furrowed in a valiant attempt to understand the complex equations that danced across the whiteboard.

Their lunch rendezvous became a cherished ritual. They would steal away to their secluded corner in the cafeteria, their conversations ranging from the intricacies of string theory to the emotional nuances of Olivia's latest piano composition. Ethan, usually reserved and quiet, found himself opening up to Olivia, sharing his dreams of unraveling the mysteries of the universe and his anxieties about the immense pressure to excel academically. Olivia, a beacon of vibrant energy, became his confidante, her unwavering support and gentle encouragement a source of strength.

One crisp afternoon, as they devoured their lunch, Olivia produced a crumpled flyer from her pocket. "There's this inter-school debate competition coming up," she announced, her eyes sparkling with excitement. "The topic is 'The Impact of Technology on Art.'"

Ethan's brows furrowed. "Debate? That's not really my forte," he mumbled, his voice laced with apprehension. Public speaking was not his forte; in fact, it was his kryptonite.

Olivia, sensing his hesitation, nudged him playfully. "Come on, Ethan," she coaxed. "Think of it as a challenge. Besides, you could be my secret weapon – the science guy who explains how technology enhances artistic expression."

A flicker of a smile played on Ethan's lips. The idea of working alongside Olivia, albeit outside his comfort zone, was strangely appealing. "Alright," he conceded, a hint of determination in his voice. "You've convinced me. But you'll have to do most of the talking."

Olivia threw her arms around him in a celebratory hug, her fiery hair tickling his cheek. "This is going to be awesome!" she exclaimed.

And so began their foray into the world of debate. Afternoons that were once spent buried in textbooks or lost in the world of music were now dedicated to researching opposing viewpoints, crafting arguments, and rehearsing rebuttals. Ethan, surprised by his own hidden talents, discovered a knack for logical reasoning and clear communication. Olivia, ever the passionate artist, poured her heart and soul into crafting a compelling argument for the positive influence of technology on art.

Their contrasting approaches proved to be a potent combination. Ethan's scientific background provided the foundation for their arguments, while Olivia's artistic flair breathed life into their presentation. Their late-night study sessions, fueled by mugs of steaming coffee and shared laughter, were a testament to their dedication and the growing bond between them.

As the excitement surrounding the debate competition intensified, so did a sense of underlying apprehension in Ethan and Olivia. While they were confident in their arguments and their ability to work together, a new challenge arose – societal expectations.

Elyria Academy, with its prestigious reputation, fostered an environment of academic rigor and social hierarchy. Students were expected to excel in their chosen fields, their interactions confined to circles of like-minded individuals. The prospect of Ethan, the quintessential bookworm, and Olivia, the flamboyant artist, collaborating on a debate was met with raised eyebrows and whispered gossip.

Their peers, blinded by societal conventions, couldn't comprehend the intellectual sparks that flew between Ethan and Olivia. They saw their collaboration as an eccentricity, a mismatch that defied the rigid social norms of the academy. Olivia, who usually thrived on attention, found herself ostracized by some classmates who disapproved of her association with Ethan, deeming him to be beneath her.

Ethan, on the other hand, faced a different kind of pressure. His peers, accustomed to his quiet demeanor and solitary pursuits, found his newfound confidence in public speaking unsettling. Rumors swirled about the reason for this sudden change, some questioning his focus on academics and others offering snide remarks about his potential motives for working with Olivia.

The whispers and judgmental glances began to chip away at Ethan's confidence. He started questioning his decision to participate in the debate, wondering if he had made a mistake in stepping outside his comfort zone. The pressure to conform, to maintain his academic standing and avoid ridicule, gnawed at him, threatening to drown out the excitement he initially felt.

Olivia, sensing his wavering resolve, confronted him one afternoon after their debate practice. "Ethan," she said, her voice filled with concern, "what's wrong? You seem distant lately."

Ethan hesitated, his gaze fixed on the floor. He didn't want to burden her with his insecurities, but the pressure was building, threatening to consume him. Finally, he confessed his anxieties, the whispers, the disapproval, and the fear of failing to live up to expectations.

Olivia listened patiently, her eyes filled with understanding. "Ethan," she said, her voice firm but gentle, "don't let them control your future. This debate is about more than just winning. It's about us, about using our unique voices to make a statement. And trust me," she added, a mischievous glint in her eyes, "together we can silence those whispers with a bang."

Ethan met her gaze, his heart warmed by her unwavering support. Olivia's confidence, her belief in both their talents, was a beacon of light in his moment of doubt. He realized that their bond transcended the petty judgments of their peers. Their friendship, built on mutual respect and intellectual curiosity, was a force to be reckoned with.

With renewed determination, Ethan and Olivia pledged to stand tall in the face of disapproval. They would use their differences not as a barrier but as a bridge, their combined intellect and creativity forming a powerful force to advocate for their beliefs. The debate competition had become more than just a competition; it was a testament to the strength of their friendship, a chance to prove to themselves and the world that true connection could blossom in the most unexpected places.

Despite their newfound resolve, the sting of disapproval continued to cast a shadow over Ethan and Olivia. The whispers in the hallways intensified, transforming from curious murmurs to snide taunts. Olivia, usually a vibrant social butterfly, found herself ostracized from her usual circles. The exclusion stung, but she refused to let it break her spirit.

Ethan, on the other hand, retreated further into his shell. The pressure to excel academically, coupled with the disapproving stares from his peers, began to affect his studies. His once meticulous notes grew cluttered, and his focus wavered during lectures. The anxieties he had confided in Olivia started to manifest in restless nights and a lack of appetite.

One evening, as the academy settled into a hushed silence after curfew, Ethan found himself seeking solace in the familiar haven of the library. He wandered aimlessly, his heart heavy with the burden of societal pressures. Just as he was about to leave, he spotted a familiar figure huddled over a piano in a secluded corner of the music room.

Olivia, her back to him, was lost in the melody flowing from her fingertips. The music, melancholic yet hopeful, resonated with his own turmoil. He stood mesmerized, the notes weaving a tapestry of emotions that mirrored his own.

As the final notes faded into the air, Olivia turned around, startled. Her eyes widened in surprise upon seeing Ethan.

"Ethan," she said, her voice laced with concern. "What are you doing here so late?"

Sensing his hesitation, Olivia beckoned him closer. He walked towards her, his shoulders slumped in defeat. Without a word, he sank onto the stool beside the piano, his head bowed.

Olivia placed a gentle hand on his shoulder. "What's wrong, Ethan?" she asked softly.

Ethan, unable to hold back the floodgates any longer, poured out his heart. He spoke of the taunts, the ostracization, and the fear of disappointing everyone, including himself.

Olivia listened patiently, her hand offering a comforting presence on his shoulder. When he finished, she spoke in a voice filled with quiet strength.

"Ethan," she said, "we can't let them win. This is about our passion, about standing up for what we believe in. Those whispers are just a reflection of their insecurities, not ours."

She took a deep breath. "You know, Ethan," she continued, a playful glint returning to her eyes, "sometimes the most brilliant ideas are born from the most unexpected combinations. Remember, it was a bookworm and an artist who came together to tackle this debate."

A flicker of a smile touched Ethan's lips. Olivia's unwavering belief in their partnership, her ability to see the silver lining even in the face of adversity, inspired him.

"You're right," he conceded, a newfound determination stirring within him. "We can't let their negativity cloud our judgment. We'll face them head-on, not with anger, but with the power of our arguments and our friendship."

Olivia smiled warmly. "That's the Ethan I know," she said, her eyes sparkling with pride. She then sat down beside him on the piano bench, and together, they played a simple melody, their fingers weaving a harmonious tapestry of strength and resilience. In that shared moment, they found solace and strength in each other's company, their friendship a beacon of light guiding them through the darkness.

The day of the debate arrived, a palpable tension hanging heavy in the air of the grand auditorium. Students buzzed with excitement, anticipation for the intellectual clash simmering beneath the surface. Ethan and Olivia, however, remained calm amidst the swirling chaos. Backstage, they huddled together, their hands clasped in a silent promise of support.

Olivia, her fiery red hair cascading down her back like a waterfall, radiated nervous energy. Yet, a determined glint shone in her emerald eyes. "Ready, Ethan?" she asked, a reassuring smile playing on her lips.

Ethan, his usual rumpled clothes ironed into a semblance of presentability, took a deep breath. "As ready as I'll ever be," he replied, his voice surprisingly steady.

Their team, a motley crew of students drawn together by their diverse viewpoints, offered them words of encouragement. In that moment, the whispers and ostracization faded away. All that mattered was the shared goal, the opportunity to showcase their combined knowledge and passion.

As their names were announced, Ethan and Olivia walked onto the stage, their contrasting appearances turning heads. Ethan, with his neatly combed hair and nervous demeanor, seemed an unlikely ally to Olivia, who stood tall and proud, her red dress a vibrant statement against the backdrop of the stage.

Their opponents, a polished pair from a rival school, presented their case first, arguing that technology stifled creativity by homogenizing art and hindering the true expression of human emotions. Ethan, listening intently, felt a surge of competitiveness mixed with a healthy dose of respect for their arguments.

When their turn came, Olivia took the lead. Her voice, initially a touch shaky, gained confidence as she spoke. She spoke of the potential of technology to expand artistic horizons, to provide new tools for expression and foster collaboration across cultures. Her passionate delivery, woven with personal anecdotes and historical references, captivated the audience.

Ethan followed, building upon Olivia's foundation. He delved into the scientific aspects of technological advancements, explaining how they could be harnessed to push the boundaries of artistic expression. He spoke with eloquence, his confidence blossoming under the scrutiny of the crowd.

Their contrasting styles, once a source of doubt, proved to be their greatest strength. Olivia's emotional appeal intertwined seamlessly with Ethan's logical reasoning, presenting a compelling and balanced argument.

The back-and-forth of rebuttals turned into an intellectual tango, their shared knowledge and passion evident in their every word. The initial whispers from their peers in the audience had transformed into murmurs of appreciation. Even the judges seemed captivated by their unique partnership.

When the final bell chimed, signaling the end of the debate, a hush fell over the auditorium. As the judges deliberated, a sense of accomplishment washed over Ethan and Olivia. They had faced their fears, defied expectations, and most importantly, they had stood together, their friendship a testament to the transformative power of connection.

Finally, the results were announced. The tension rose exponentially until the judge declared, "The winners of this debate are Ethan Moore and Olivia Thompson from Elyria Academy!"

A wave of cheers erupted from the audience, punctuated by surprised gasps and enthusiastic shouts. Ethan and Olivia, overwhelmed with a mix of relief and exhilaration, shared a warm embrace on stage. In that moment, the whispers and doubts of their peers seemed insignificant. They had overcome the societal pressures, proving that intellectual brilliance could bloom in the most unexpected places.

The debate wasn't just a victory; it was a turning point. As they walked off the stage, hand in hand, the whispers around them had transformed into murmurs of respect and admiration. Their journey, fueled by friendship and a shared passion for knowledge, had just begun. The vast canvas of their future, once clouded by societal expectations, now held the promise of endless possibilities, a testament to the extraordinary connection that blossomed between a bookworm and an artist in the hallowed halls of Elyria Academy.

Chapter 3: Facing Trials and Tribulations, Their Love Grows Stronger

The victory at the inter-school debate propelled Ethan and Olivia into the spotlight. Their names were etched on the academy newsletter, their picture plastered beneath the bold headline, "Elyria Academy Triumphs in Debate Competition." Whispers that once aimed to belittle their collaboration now morphed into murmurs of admiration. Even their professors, accustomed to seeing them excel in their respective fields, were pleasantly surprised by the synergy they displayed on stage.

However, the newfound fame didn't alter the core of their relationship. They cherished their stolen moments in the library, Ethan engrossed in explaining the intricacies of black holes while Olivia filled the silent void with her melodic improvisations. Lunchtime rendezvous continued, their conversations venturing beyond the confines of science and art, delving into the murky waters of personal aspirations and hidden vulnerabilities.

One crisp December evening, with the first snowflakes swirling in the air, Ethan found himself drawn to the familiar refuge of the astronomy club meeting. Olivia, ever the punctual one, wasn't there yet. He stood by the telescope, gazing up at the star-studded sky, a sense of unease settling in his stomach.

He had spent the past week in a state of turmoil, a knot of unarticulated emotions tightening his chest whenever Olivia was around. Her fiery spirit, her infectious laughter, and her unwavering support – all conspired to create a feeling that transcended the boundaries of friendship.

As Ethan contemplated his newfound feelings, Olivia burst through the observatory door, a flurry of activity. "Ethan, I'm so sorry I'm late!" she exclaimed, her cheeks flushed from the brisk walk. "The practice session with the school band ran longer than expected."

Ethan managed a smile, his gaze lingering on her a beat longer than necessary. "No worries," he mumbled, the knot in his stomach twisting tighter.

The meeting progressed, but Ethan's mind remained preoccupied. He found himself stealing glances at Olivia, his heart skipping a beat whenever their eyes met. The once-familiar constellations seemed to lose their brilliance, overshadowed by the turmoil brewing within him.

After the meeting, as they walked back towards the academy, the silence between them was deafening. Ethan wrestled with his internal conflict, his mind searching for the right words to express the overwhelming emotions churning within him.

Finally, he stopped abruptly, causing Olivia to bump into him. "Ethan? What's wrong?" she asked, her brow furrowed in concern.

Ethan took a deep breath, his gaze fixed on the snow-covered path. "Olivia," he began, his voice barely a whisper, "there's something I need to tell you."

He poured his heart out, his voice trembling slightly as he confessed his feelings, his admiration for her intelligence and passion morphing into something deeper. His words tumbled out in a torrent, revealing his fears of being rejected and his hopes that their connection was more than just a newfound friendship.

Olivia listened intently, her vibrant red hair creating a stark contrast against the white backdrop of the falling snow. As Ethan finished his confession, a silence descended, filled only by the gentle crunching of their footsteps on the snowy path.

Ethan, his heart pounding against his ribs, braced himself for whatever response she might have. He had bared his soul, and now, his future hung in the precarious balance of her answer.

The silence stretched on, thick with anticipation. Ethan dared to steal a glance at Olivia, his heart sinking at the unreadable expression on her face. Was it surprise? Hesitation? Rejection? The possibilities swirled in his mind, each one more agonizing than the last.

Just when his anxieties threatened to consume him, Olivia spoke. Her voice, a soft whisper, surprised him. "Ethan," she began, "to be honest, I... I had no idea you felt this way."

A flicker of hope ignited within him. "No?" he stammered, a hint of disbelief coloring his voice.

Olivia shook her head, a hesitant smile gracing her lips. "Truth be told, I've been feeling something different too. Your support, your curiosity, they made me see the world in a new light. You challenged me to think beyond the notes, to explore the science behind the music."

Ethan's heart soared. The knot in his stomach loosened, replaced by a warmth that spread through his entire being. "You mean..." he began, his voice thick with emotion.

"Maybe," Olivia interrupted with a playful twinkle in her eyes. "The stars weren't the only ones aligning tonight, Ethan."

A wave of relief washed over him, followed by a surge of exhilaration. He had confessed his feelings, and to his immense joy, they weren't one-sided. A new chapter in their relationship was unfolding, a breathtaking vista of possibilities stretching before them like a star-studded sky.

They stood there for a moment, the weight of unspoken words hanging heavy in the air. The falling snow, once a backdrop to Ethan's anxieties, now seemed to sparkle with a newfound magic.

"So," Ethan finally managed, his voice tinged with a nervous excitement, "what does this mean for us?"

Olivia's smile widened. "Well," she said, her eyes twinkling with mischief, "it means we can explore this new constellation, together."

Ethan's heart skipped a beat. Together. The word resonated within him, a promise of shared experiences and a future filled with wonder. They were no longer just a bookworm and an artist, their contrasting passions now intertwined. They were explorers, venturing into the uncharted territory of love, their journey guided by the light of their newfound connection.

With a newfound confidence, Ethan reached out and took Olivia's hand. Her touch sent a jolt of electricity through him, grounding him in the present moment. They stood there, hands clasped beneath the starlit sky, the universe mirroring the immensity of the emotions swirling within them.

The path ahead may have been uncertain, but they faced it together, their friendship blossoming into something far more profound. The academy walls, once a barrier, now seemed to shrink away, replaced by the vast expanse of possibilities that lay before them. Their love story, born from a chance encounter amidst the towering shelves of the library, had taken a momentous turn. The stars, once silent observers, now seemed to wink in approval, their celestial glow a testament to the extraordinary connection that illuminated the lives of Ethan and Olivia.

The revelation under the starlit sky marked a new chapter in Ethan and Olivia's relationship. Gone was the awkwardness of unspoken feelings, replaced by a comfortable intimacy that bloomed naturally. Stolen glances became lingering touches, shy smiles morphed into shared laughter, and their conversations flowed effortlessly, infused with a newfound layer of meaning.

However, navigating the uncharted territory of love wasn't without its challenges. Ethan, accustomed to the solitude of his studies, found himself yearning for Olivia's presence constantly. He struggled to maintain focus during lectures, his mind wandering to stolen moments of laughter or the warmth of her hand in his. Olivia, in turn, discovered a newfound possessiveness, a desire for Ethan's undivided attention that clashed with her independent spirit.

One afternoon, as they sat huddled in their usual corner of the cafeteria, Olivia's brow furrowed in concentration. Her fingers tapped rhythmically on the table, a habit that surfaced whenever she was composing. "Hey," Ethan said, nudging her playfully. "What are you working on?"

Olivia glanced up, a mischievous glint in her eyes. "It's a secret," she teased, tucking a stray strand of hair behind her ear.

Ethan's heart skipped a beat. Secrets, once a non-issue in their friendship, now held a different weight. He yearned to be a part of her creative process, to share the joy of her artistic endeavors. The possessiveness he'd been battling since their confession reared its ugly head.

"But we share everything," he stammered, his voice laced with a hint of disappointment.

Olivia's smile faltered. "Not everything, Ethan," she countered gently. "Everyone needs a little space to create, to nurture their own voice."

Ethan felt a pang of guilt. He knew she was right. His need for constant companionship wasn't fair to her artistic spirit. He offered a sheepish grin. "You're right. Sorry, I overstepped."

Olivia's smile returned, full of understanding. "Don't worry about it," she said, squeezing his hand reassuringly. "Just promise me you'll be the first one to hear it when it's finished."

Ethan nodded eagerly, his possessiveness momentarily overshadowed by his excitement at the prospect of hearing her secret melody. The incident, however, served as a wake-up call. Their relationship, while strong, required a delicate balance between intimacy and individuality.

The days that followed were filled with a newfound understanding. Ethan, respecting Olivia's need for creative space, focused on his studies, channeling his anxieties into exploring complex scientific theories. Olivia, energized by the budding romance, poured her heart into her music, the secret melody a testament to the emotions swirling within her.

One evening, as Ethan finished his homework in the library, a familiar melody drifted through the air. It was the secret melody, a hauntingly beautiful piece that resonated with a depth of emotion he hadn't expected. He followed the sound to the music room, finding Olivia bathed in the warm glow of a solitary lamp, her fingers dancing across the piano keys.

As the final notes faded into the air, Olivia turned around, a shy smile gracing her lips. "Ethan," she said, her voice barely a whisper.

He walked towards her, his heart swelling with a mix of awe and emotion. "It's beautiful, Olivia," he said, his voice thick with sincerity. "More beautiful than anything I've ever heard."

Olivia's cheeks flushed with a blush. "It's about you," she confessed, her voice barely above a whisper. "About the way you see the world, about the universe reflected in your eyes."

Ethan was speechless. The melody, a tapestry of emotions, mirrored his own feelings for Olivia. It was a love letter in musical form, a testament to the profound connection they shared. In that moment, amidst the quiet grandeur of the music room, their love story transcended words, reaching a new level of understanding and intimacy.

The secret melody, born from Olivia's creative solitude, became a symbol of their evolving relationship. It was a reminder that while they were bound by a powerful connection, their individual passions and dreams enriched their journey together. The stars, their silent companions, continued to witness the blossoming of their love, a testament to the extraordinary union of a bookworm and an artist, forever linked by the invisible threads of science, art, and the boundless universe of their hearts.

NEWS OF ETHAN AND OLIVIA'S relationship spread like wildfire through the hallowed halls of Elyria Academy. Initial whispers of surprise quickly morphed into genuine congratulations. Even their former doubters couldn't help but be charmed by the obvious happiness radiating from the couple.

The newfound romance, however, presented a new set of challenges. While their shared passion for knowledge remained a cornerstone of their connection, their academic pursuits began to diverge. Ethan, fueled by a renewed enthusiasm, delved deeper into astrophysics, his nights consumed by studying complex mathematical models and theoretical frameworks. Olivia, meanwhile, embarked on composing her first original piece, a grand orchestral symphony inspired by the vastness of the universe and the intricacies of human connection.

Their once-synchronized study sessions became a thing of the past. Ethan's conversations were peppered with jargon about gravitational waves and quantum entanglement, leaving Olivia's head spinning. Olivia, in turn, obsessed with finding the perfect notes to capture the emotions swirling within her, would spend hours lost in the world of music theory, oblivious to Ethan's presence beside her.

The initial glow of romance began to dim, replaced by a sense of quiet frustration. Ethan longed for Olivia's undivided attention, the intellectual sparring sessions that once fueled their connection. Olivia, in turn, yearned for Ethan's presence, a simple conversation that didn't require deciphering scientific code.

One particularly trying evening, as Ethan battled a particularly complex equation, frustration boiled over. "Olivia," he said, his voice laced with irritation, "could you please keep it down a bit? I'm trying to concentrate."

Olivia, engrossed in composing a particularly dramatic crescendo, flinched at his sharp tone. She slammed her laptop shut, her brow furrowed. "And I'm trying to create," she retorted, her voice equally sharp.

The silence that followed was heavy with unspoken hurt. Ethan realized the error of his ways. Olivia's passion for music deserved his full support, just as his pursuit of astrophysics deserved hers. He apologized for his outburst, expressing his admiration for her dedication.

Olivia, understanding his frustration, offered a conciliatory smile. "Maybe," she suggested, "we need a new approach."

And so, a new routine was born. Ethan, armed with a renewed appreciation for Olivia's artistry, started attending her orchestra rehearsals. He sat captivated by the symphony taking shape, his scientific mind appreciating the intricate harmonies and the emotional power of music. Olivia, in turn, began accompanying Ethan to stargazing sessions. She listened intently as he explained the constellations and the mysteries of the universe, her artistic spirit finding inspiration in the vastness of space.

Their individual pursuits, once a source of friction, became a way to enrich their connection. They learned to celebrate each other's passions, offering support and encouragement even when they didn't fully understand the details. Their love story became a beautiful symphony, a harmonious blend of science and art, a testament to the strength that could be found in supporting each other's dreams.

As graduation loomed on the horizon, Ethan and Olivia stood at the precipice of their future. Their paths would diverge, leading them to prestigious universities across the country. But the foundation of their love, built on respect, understanding, and a shared passion for exploration, was strong. They knew, with unwavering certainty, that the distance wouldn't diminish the melody of their love story. The stars, their silent witnesses, would continue to guide them, as they embarked on a new chapter, their hearts forever entwined in the cosmic dance of love and knowledge.

Chapter 4: The Unveiling of Secrets and the Revelation of True Identities

Years had passed since Ethan and Olivia's emotional goodbye at Elyria Academy. Graduation had marked the bittersweet end of an era, their paths diverging as they pursued their dreams at universities on opposite sides of the country. Yet, the distance couldn't sever the bond they shared. Letters, filled with heartfelt confessions and scientific musings, became their lifeline, a bridge across the miles.

Ethan, now a thriving undergraduate at the California Institute of Technology, thrived in the vibrant intellectual atmosphere. Surrounded by brilliant minds, he delved deeper into the mysteries of the cosmos, his research focusing on the elusive concept of dark matter. His nights were filled with poring over complex data sets, searching for patterns that could unlock the secrets of the universe's missing mass.

Olivia, blossoming in the prestigious Juilliard School of Music, embraced the world of composition. Her days were a whirlwind of composing sessions, orchestra rehearsals, and late-night practice sessions where she honed her skills on the piano. Her once-shy melodies evolved into powerful compositions, infused with the emotions of separation and the yearning for connection.

Despite their busy schedules, they carved out time for each other. Weekly video calls became a cherished ritual, a window into each other's lives. Ethan would share his frustrations with a particularly stubborn equation, his face lighting up as Olivia, ever the optimist, offered words of encouragement. Olivia, in turn, would describe the challenges of translating emotions into music, her voice filled with excitement as she played snippets of her newest composition for Ethan's eager ears.

The distance, however, wasn't without its challenges. Loneliness gnawed at the edges of their happiness. The simple act of holding hands or sharing a laugh under the starlit sky became a distant memory. The constant stream of letters and video calls couldn't fully replicate the warmth of physical presence.

One particularly gloomy November evening, as a relentless rain lashed against his dorm window, Ethan found himself battling a wave of despair. He missed Olivia's laugh, the comfort of her presence, the way she challenged him to see the world from a different perspective. He picked up his pen, his usual enthusiasm for writing dampened by the weight of his emotions.

Struggling to articulate his heartache, he poured his feelings onto the page. Words tumbled out, expressing his longing for Olivia, his unwavering belief in their connection, and his fear that the distance might eventually dim the flame of their love. Sealing the letter with a heavy sigh, he dropped it into the mailbox, the rain mirroring the storm brewing within him.

DAYS STRETCHED INTO weeks, and Ethan received no reply from Olivia. The silence gnawed at him, his anxieties multiplying with each passing day. Had his letter, a torrent of raw emotions, scared her away? Had the distance finally taken its toll on their relationship?

He found solace in his research, burying himself in complex calculations and data analysis. Yet, even amidst the constellations of scientific theories, Olivia's absence echoed in the void. He missed the way she could translate the complexities of the universe into a melody that resonated with his soul.

One crisp December evening, as Ethan stepped out of the library after a particularly grueling study session, his phone buzzed in his pocket. It was an email notification. His heart skipped a beat as he saw the sender's name – Olivia. With trembling fingers, he clicked it open.

It wasn't a letter, but a link. He clicked it, his breath catching in his throat as a video began to play. The screen displayed a breathtaking scene – a concert hall bathed in the warm glow of the stage lights. An orchestra sat poised, instruments gleaming under the spotlights.

Then, Olivia appeared, radiant in a flowing white dress. She raised her baton, a confident smile gracing her lips. As the music began, Ethan felt a surge of emotions wash over him. It was her symphony, the one she had been composing for months, the one she had shared snippets of during their video calls.

But this wasn't just any performance. The music, a tapestry of emotions, mirrored the journey of their love story. The opening notes, melancholic and yearning, spoke of their separation. The tempo picked up, weaving in a sense of determination and hope. The melody soared, reaching a crescendo that resonated with the depth of their connection. The final notes faded, leaving a lingering sense of peace and a promise of a future reunion.

Tears welled up in Ethan's eyes as the video ended. It was a love letter in musical form, a response to his anxieties, a testament to the enduring strength of their bond. He knew, with a certainty that transcended distance, that their love story wasn't over. It was simply a new chapter, waiting to be written.

The next morning, his inbox held another email from Olivia. It was short and sweet, containing just a single sentence: "Book a flight, Ethan. The stars are waiting for us."

A smile bloomed on Ethan's face, as bright as the constellations he spent years studying. He knew exactly what he had to do. Distance may have tested their love, but it couldn't sever the connection forged under the starlit sky. Their symphony, a beautiful blend of science and art, would continue to play, its melody carrying them towards a future filled with love, music, and the endless wonders of the universe.

Reunited under the familiar glow of the stage lights, Ethan and Olivia reveled in their long-awaited embrace. The physical separation, a source of constant worry, melted away as they held each other close. In that moment, their love story wasn't just rekindled, it was reborn, stronger and more vibrant than ever before.

Over steaming cups of coffee in a cozy cafe near the concert hall, they shared stories and dreams. Ethan spoke of his research, his voice filled with excitement as he explained his latest breakthrough in dark matter detection. Olivia, in turn, described the inspiration behind her symphony, the way their connection had fueled her creativity.

As they talked, a new realization dawned on them. The distance, while challenging, had also opened doors to new perspectives. Ethan's research had taken on a new dimension, infused with the emotional depth he gleaned from Olivia's music. Olivia's compositions, once focused on individual emotions, now held a broader resonance, reflecting the vastness of the universe Ethan explored.

Their individual journeys, enriched by their time apart, had become beautifully intertwined. They were no longer just Ethan the astrophysicist and Olivia the musician; they were partners, collaborators, each one a reflection of the other's dreams.

The future stretched before them, a universe of possibilities waiting to be explored. They envisioned a future where Ethan's scientific discoveries would inspire Olivia's musical compositions, and Olivia's music would provide a soulful lens through which Ethan could view the cosmos.

With a newfound determination, they began to make plans. Ethan, resolute in his desire to be closer to Olivia, applied for research positions at universities on the East Coast. Olivia, her heart set on a career as a professional composer, started networking with renowned orchestras and music producers.

The path ahead wouldn't be easy. There would be challenges, sacrifices, and moments of doubt. But as they walked hand-in-hand under the starlit sky that night, they knew they could face anything, as long as they faced it together. The universe, their silent witness, seemed to shimmer with approval, its vast expanse mirroring the boundless love and potential that resided within them.

Their journey, once a simple love story between a bookworm and an artist, had blossomed into an epic saga of love, ambition, and the beautiful tapestry woven between science and art. As they gazed at the stars, their hearts overflowing with hope, they knew that their symphony, a testament to their enduring connection, would continue to play its melody for years to come.

Months turned into years, and Ethan and Olivia's love story continued to unfold like a captivating melody. Ethan secured a prestigious research position at a university near Juilliard, allowing him to pursue his astrophysics research while being close to Olivia. Olivia, fueled by her newfound inspiration, landed a coveted position as a composer-in-residence with a renowned orchestra.

Their lives, once separate narratives, became a beautiful counterpoint. Ethan would spend his days deciphering the mysteries of the universe, his mind ablaze with complex equations and theoretical frameworks. Olivia, meanwhile, would lose herself in the world of music, her fingers dancing across the piano keys, translating emotions and scientific concepts into breathtaking compositions.

Their evenings were a testament to their enduring connection. They would gather in their cozy apartment, Ethan sharing his latest research breakthroughs with a childlike wonder, while Olivia, captivated by his passion, would translate his scientific jargon into metaphors woven from music theory. In turn, Olivia would play snippets of her latest compositions, her melodies painting sonic landscapes that mirrored the vastness of space Ethan explored.

Their collaboration wasn't limited to their personal lives. Ethan, inspired by Olivia's music, began incorporating artistic elements into his research presentations. He used musical analogies to explain complex scientific concepts, making his work more accessible and engaging for a broader audience. Olivia, in turn, started incorporating scientific themes into her compositions. Her music, once purely emotional, now held a deeper resonance, reflecting the awe-inspiring beauty and intricate mechanics of the universe.

One evening, as they sat nestled together on their couch, a news notification popped up on Ethan's phone. It was an announcement for a prestigious science symposium, with a call for proposals that combined scientific exploration with artistic expression.

Ethan and Olivia exchanged a glance, a silent understanding passing between them. This was their chance, a platform to showcase the unique synergy of their individual strengths, a testament to the power of their love story.

Over the next few weeks, their apartment transformed into a creative haven. Scientific diagrams mingled with sheet music, equations danced alongside musical notations, and the air buzzled with their shared enthusiasm. They spent nights lost in passionate discussions, weaving together scientific theories with musical principles, their love for each other fueling their creative fire.

Finally, the day of the symposium arrived. Ethan and Olivia presented their proposal, a groundbreaking exploration of the universe using a blend of scientific research and musical composition. Their presentation captivated the audience, the scientific accuracy intertwined with the emotional depth of Olivia's music creating a truly awe-inspiring experience.

The symposium ended with a standing ovation. Ethan and Olivia, their hands intertwined, stood on stage, their hearts brimming with pride. They had not only impressed the scientific community but also shown the world the power of love, collaboration, and the beautiful bridge that could be built between science and art.

Their journey, once a chance encounter amidst the towering shelves of a library, had evolved into a symphony of second chances, a testament to the enduring power of love and the boundless possibilities that unfolded when hearts and minds dared to dream together. As they stepped off the stage, hand in hand, they knew that their love story, like the universe they explored, was a never-ending exploration, a melody that would continue to play for years to come, forever echoing under the vast and shimmering canvas of the stars.

Chapter 5: The Enduring Legacy: A Love Story for the Ages

Years had etched their passage on Ethan and Olivia. Gone were the youthful anxieties and uncertainties that had colored their early days together. In their place resided a quiet confidence, a deep understanding forged in the crucible of shared dreams and unwavering support.

Their careers had blossomed, mirroring the trajectory of their love story. Ethan, a renowned astrophysicist, had made significant contributions to the field of dark matter research. His innovative approach, blending scientific rigor with artistic expression, had garnered him widespread acclaim. Olivia, a celebrated composer, had captivated audiences worldwide with her symphonies that weaved together the beauty of the cosmos with the complexities of human emotions.

Despite their success, their lives weren't without challenges. The demands of their careers often pushed them to their limits, leaving them with limited time for each other. Ethan, engrossed in groundbreaking research projects, would spend nights poring over data sets and complex simulations. Olivia, traveling the world with renowned orchestras, navigated the rigorous schedules and demanding rehearsals of a professional musician.

One particularly busy summer, their communication dwindled. Emails went unanswered, phone calls missed. The once-vibrant melody of their daily conversations fell silent, replaced by the relentless hum of their individual pursuits.

A sense of unease settled in Ethan's stomach as he sat in his cluttered office, surrounded by astronomical charts and research papers. The familiar glow of his computer screen felt strangely cold and isolating. He glanced at the picture frame on his desk, a photograph of him and Olivia, younger and carefree, their eyes sparkling with shared dreams. A pang of guilt washed over him.

He reached for his phone, his finger hovering over Olivia's contact. Should he call? Would she even pick up, given her demanding schedule? The uncertainty held him back, a fear of disrupting her focus and further straining their connection.

Meanwhile, Olivia sat backstage in a concert hall in a bustling European city. The pre-performance jitters gnawed at her, a familiar mix of excitement and nervousness. As she ran through her scales on the piano, her fingers brushed against a worn silver locket she always wore. Inside, nestled against a faded photograph, was a small piece of paper – a snippet of a melody scrawled in Ethan's hand, a reminder of their early days, filled with shared laughter and stargazing sessions.

A wave of nostalgia washed over her. She missed their late-night conversations, their passionate debates about science and art, the simple comfort of his presence. The silence surrounding her, once a necessary solitude for her creative process, now felt deafening.

The final call echoed through the hall, signaling the start of the performance. Olivia took a deep breath, pushing her anxieties aside. As she raised her baton, the melody that danced in her mind wasn't the planned symphony, but a soft, melancholic tune, a melody born from the echoes of a love story yearning for reconnection.

The concert ended with a polite applause, a stark contrast to the usual thunderous ovations Olivia had come to expect. The poignant melody, filled with a longing that resonated with the audience, had left them stunned and introspective. Backstage, a sense of unease gnawed at Olivia. The performance, a stark departure from her usual style, had exposed a vulnerability she hadn't intended to share.

Exhausted yet restless, Olivia retreated to her hotel room. The silence felt heavy, a mirror reflecting the growing distance between her and Ethan. She picked up the locket, tracing the worn silver with her thumb. A tear escaped her eye, landing on the faded photograph of them, their youthful smiles a stark contrast to the growing distance she felt in her heart.

Unable to shake off the feeling of disconnection, Olivia decided to take a leap of faith. Pulling out her laptop, she logged in to their shared online journal, a virtual space where they had documented their dreams, anxieties, and inspirations throughout their relationship.

The last entry, dated several months prior, was from Ethan. It spoke of his latest research breakthrough, his excitement tinged with a subtle note of loneliness. Olivia felt a pang of guilt. Had she been so consumed by her own career that she'd failed to acknowledge his struggles?

Tears welling up in her eyes, she began to type. Her words flowed freely, expressing her love, her anxieties, and a deep longing for reconnection. She spoke of the concert, how the melody had emerged from a subconscious yearning for their shared past.

Finishing with a shaky breath, she clicked "post," sending the entry into the digital ether. A sliver of hope flickered within her. Maybe, just maybe, this vulnerable act could bridge the growing distance between them.

Meanwhile, Ethan, plagued by similar anxieties, was staring at the photograph on his desk. The unanswered emails, the missed calls, all echoed in his mind. With a heavy heart, he opened their shared journal. Finding Olivia's new entry, he devoured her words, his heart pounding with a mixture of relief and sorrow.

He realized that his single-minded focus on research had blinded him to Olivia's needs. The loneliness he felt wasn't a one-way street. Shame washed over him, coupled with a fierce determination to mend the rift he had unknowingly created.

Picking up his pen, he responded to Olivia's entry, his words filled with heartfelt apologies, a renewed sense of appreciation for their connection, and a proposal that echoed Olivia's own longing. He suggested a trip, a journey back to Elyria Academy, the place where their love story had begun.

Hours later, as the first rays of dawn painted the sky, a notification popped up on Olivia's phone. It was Ethan's reply. A bittersweet smile spread across her face as she began to read. The universe, in its own mysterious way, seemed to be nudging them back towards each other, offering them a chance to rediscover the melody of their love story amidst the familiar echoes of their past.

The crisp autumn air of New England carried a faint scent of nostalgia as Ethan and Olivia stepped back onto the familiar grounds of Elyria Academy. Years had passed since their graduation, but the towering brick buildings and sprawling lawns seemed frozen in time, a silent witness to their youthful dreams and burgeoning love.

They walked hand-in-hand, a comfortable silence settling between them. The weight of their unspoken anxieties hung in the air, a stark contrast to the carefree chatter of their past visits. They reached their favorite spot – the hilltop overlooking the campus, the same spot where they had first shared their dreams under the starlit sky.

As they stood gazing at the familiar landscape, a sense of vulnerability washed over Olivia. "Ethan," she began, her voice barely a whisper, "I'm so sorry. My career, my ambition – they took over. I forgot about us, about the melody we created together."

Ethan turned to her, his eyes filled with empathy. "Olivia," he said, his voice gentle, "It wasn't just you. My research consumed me. I forgot that science thrives on collaboration, just like love."

A tear rolled down Olivia's cheek, catching the moonlight. "Can we rewrite the melody?" she asked, her voice laced with hope.

Ethan reached out, wiping the tear away with his thumb. "We can certainly try," he said, a smile gracing his lips.

As the night deepened, they sat nestled together, lost in conversation. They reminisced about their shared past, the awkward glances exchanged in the library, the thrill of their first stargazing session, the symphony Olivia had composed that mirrored his scientific fascination with the universe.

As they talked, the silence that had strained their connection began to melt away. They realized their individual journeys, while consuming, had ultimately enriched their shared passion. Olivia's music had become more grounded, infused with a scientific precision that resonated with Ethan's research. Ethan's presentations, once sterile and technical, now incorporated captivating metaphors borrowed from the world of music.

As the first stars began to twinkle in the vast expanse of the night sky, Ethan reached into his pocket and pulled out a small, velvet box. Olivia's breath hitched as she saw what lay nestled within – a delicate silver ring engraved with a musical note and a constellation pattern.

"Olivia," Ethan began, his voice thick with emotion, "You are the melody that plays in the silence of my universe. Will you continue writing this symphony with me?"

Tears welled up in Olivia's eyes, a radiant smile breaking through. "Yes, Ethan," she whispered, her voice choked with emotion. "Yes, a thousand times yes."

As they slipped the rings onto each other's fingers, a shooting star streaked across the sky, leaving a trail of shimmering light. It was a cosmic sign, a promise whispered by the universe. Their love story, once a duet on the verge of becoming a discordant harmony, had found its rhythm again. Under the endless canvas of the night sky, they stood together, two souls intertwined by science, art, and the enduring melody of their love.

News of Ethan and Olivia's renewed commitment spread like wildfire through the hallowed halls of Elyria Academy. Former classmates, their faces etched with the passage of time, greeted them with warm embraces and well wishes. Professors, who had nurtured their early love of learning, beamed with pride, their eyes twinkling with the knowledge that sometimes, the most profound discoveries weren't found in textbooks, but in the depths of the human heart.

Their return to Elyria Academy wasn't just a sentimental journey; it was a catalyst for a new chapter in their lives. Inspired by their shared vision, they proposed a revolutionary program – a curriculum that blended scientific inquiry with artistic expression.

Ethan, drawing on Olivia's musical compositions, devised a series of lectures that used musical analogies to explain complex scientific concepts. Students, captivated by the unique approach, found themselves grappling with the mysteries of dark matter and the intricacies of quantum mechanics, their imaginations ignited by the evocative power of music.

Olivia, in turn, incorporated scientific themes into her music workshops. Her students, guided by her expertise, composed pieces that reflected the awe-inspiring beauty of the cosmos, the celestial dance of planets, the birth and death of stars. The once-segregated disciplines of science and art began to converge, weaving a tapestry of knowledge that resonated with both the analytical and creative sides of the human mind.

Their program, a testament to the synergy of their love story, became a beacon of innovation at Elyria Academy. Students from all disciplines flocked to their classes, their minds buzzing with newfound possibilities. The once-familiar classrooms transformed into vibrant spaces where creativity and scientific rigor danced hand-in-hand.

One evening, as Ethan and Olivia sat on the familiar hilltop, bathed in the warm glow of the setting sun, they watched a group of students huddled around a telescope, their faces alight with curiosity. A young woman, her voice filled with excitement, pointed out a constellation, its name echoing a melody from Olivia's latest composition.

Ethan turned to Olivia, a contented smile gracing his lips. "We did it, didn't we?" he whispered.

Olivia leaned her head against his shoulder, a tear of joy rolling down her cheek. "We did," she replied, her voice filled with pride. "We wrote a new melody, not just for ourselves, but for all those who dare to dream with both their hearts and minds."

The universe, vast and ever-expanding, stretched before them. It was a universe that had witnessed the birth and death of stars, the evolution of life, and the enduring power of love. In its infinite wisdom, it had brought Ethan and Olivia together, reminding them that the greatest discoveries, both scientific and artistic, often lay at the intersection of curiosity, collaboration, and the enduring melody of the human spirit. As they sat there, hand in hand, their love story, a symphony reborn, echoed through the halls of Elyria Academy, a testament to the boundless potential that unfolded when hearts dared to dream together.

Conclusion

Years after their reunion at Elyria Academy, Ethan and Olivia's love story continued to inspire and transform lives. Their program, a testament to the synergy of their love, had become a global phenomenon, revolutionizing education and igniting a passion for STEM in countless young minds.

Ethan, revered for his groundbreaking research and innovative teaching methods, continued to explore the mysteries of the cosmos, his work fueled by Olivia's musical compositions that echoed the language of the universe. Olivia, a celebrated composer and mentor, composed symphonies that captured the essence of scientific discoveries, her melodies weaving together the beauty of the natural world and the wonders of human ingenuity.

Their love, a beacon of light amidst the vast expanse of the universe, had shown the world that science and art weren't opposing forces, but rather complementary halves of a single, harmonious whole. Their story, a testament to the power of love, creativity, and collaboration, served as an inspiration to all who dared to dream beyond the boundaries of their perceived limitations.

As they stood hand-in-hand, gazing at the starlit sky, their hearts filled with gratitude, they knew that their love story was far from over. It was an ongoing symphony, a continuous exploration of the infinite possibilities that lay at the intersection of science, art, and the boundless potential of the human spirit.

A Note to the Reader

Dear Reader,

As you close the final page of "Cosmic Melodies; A Duet of Love and Discovery," I hope you find yourself lingering in the echoes of Ethan and Olivia's extraordinary love story. Their journey, a testament to the power of love, creativity, and collaboration, has undoubtedly left an indelible mark on your heart and mind.

In the vast expanse of the cosmos, where science and art intertwine, Ethan and Olivia's love story unfolded, a symphony of passion, discovery, and unwavering dedication. Their shared journey, a testament to the boundless potential that lies at the intersection of different perspectives, serves as an inspiration to all who dare to dream beyond the confines of their perceived limitations.

As you embark on your own life's symphony, remember the melodies that resonated within you throughout this story:

* The melody of love: Let love be the guiding force in your life, the compass that directs you towards meaningful connections and unwavering support.

* The melody of creativity: Nurture your creative spirit, allowing it to flourish and express itself in unique and inspiring ways.

* The melody of collaboration: Seek out opportunities to collaborate with others, sharing your knowledge, talents, and perspectives to create something extraordinary.

* The melody of discovery: Embrace the spirit of discovery, venturing beyond the familiar to explore new horizons and expand your understanding of the world around you.

May Ethan and Olivia's love story serve as a beacon of light, illuminating your path as you navigate the complexities and wonders of life. Remember, the greatest discoveries, both scientific and artistic, often lie at the intersection of curiosity, collaboration, and the enduring melody of the human spirit.

WITH GRATITUDE,
Mrigendra Bharti

About the Author

Mrigendra Bharti, born on June 29, 2004, in South Delhi, India, is a multifaceted individual recognized as the owner of Mrigendra Bharti Group InfoTech India Co. Pvt Ltd. Beyond his entrepreneurial endeavors, he is a distinguished music producer, director, and a budding writer.

Embarking on his professional journey at a young age, Mrigendra Bharti's visionary leadership has led to the establishment of several successful ventures, including Croma Music Series Entertainment, Sellbrochure, Fauget Innovative, and more.

What sets Mrigendra apart is his early initiation into the world of business. His foray into the unknown realms of entrepreneurship began during his 10th-grade years, where he delved into the music industry. This initial venture laid the foundation for subsequent achievements, showcasing his dedication and resilience.

Having honed his skills in music, Mrigendra Bharti not only demonstrated significant growth in his craft but also expanded his professional network. His passion extends beyond music, encompassing app and website development, as well as graphic design.

Fueled by his creative aspirations, Mrigendra established the Mrigendra Bharti Group, a company specializing in website and app development. Currently, he collaborates with a dedicated team, collectively working on ambitious projects that promise innovation and excellence.

Mrigendra's journey serves as an inspiration, particularly for today's students, highlighting the potential of youthful determination and the ability to transform innovative ideas into successful businesses. As he continues to make strides in various domains, Mrigendra Bharti remains a dynamic force, contributing vibrancy to the realms of business, music, and technology.

Read more at https://www.imwriter-mrigendra.rf.gd.